Make Way for Readers

For Linda Brodie

—J. S.

SIMON & SCHUSTER BOOKS FOR YOUNG READERS
An imprint of Simon & Schuster Children's Publishing Division • 1230 Avenue of the Americas, New York, New York 10020

For information about special discounts for bulk purchases, please contact Simon & Schuster Special Sales at 1-866-506-1949 or business@simonandschuster.com.
The Simon & Schuster Speakers Bureau can bring authors to your live event. For more information or to book an event, contact the Simon & Schuster Speakers Bureau at 1-866-248-3049 or visit our website at www.simonspeakers.com.
Book design by Chloë Foglia • The text for this book was set in Garamond. • The illustrations for this book were rendered in colored pencils.
Manufactured in China
0416 SCP
2 4 6 8 10 9 7 5 3 1
Library of Congress Cataloging-in-Publication Data
Names: Sierra, Judy. | Karas, G. Brian, illustrator.
Title: Make way for readers / Judy Sierra ; illustrated by G. Brian Karas.
Description: First edition. | New York : Simon & Schuster Books for Young Readers, [2016] | "A Paula Wiseman book." | Summary: Animal toddlers arrive for storytime with Miss Bingo the flamingo.
Identifiers: LCCN 2014011224 |
ISBN 9781481418515 (hardcover) | ISBN 9781481418522 (eBook)
Subjects: | CYAC: Stories in rhyme. | Books and reading—Fiction. |
Toddlers—Fiction. | Animals—Fiction.
Classification: LCC PZ8.3.S577 Mak 2015 | DDC [E]—dc23 LC record available at http://lccn.loc.gov/2014011224

MAKE WAY FOR READERS

Judy Sierra

Illustrated by G. Brian Karas

A Paula Wiseman Book
Simon & Schuster Books for Young Readers
NEW YORK LONDON TORONTO SYDNEY NEW DELHI

Make way for the readers,
the riders, the rollers,
arriving in backpacks,
on bikes, and in strollers.

Emma and Rufus
find books about bunnies.
Rory and Annabelle
read something funny.

Now everyone listens
to merry Miss Bingo,
the storytime rhymer,
the singing flamingo.

Three little kittens lost their mittens
and they began to cry
Little Miss Muffet sat on her tuffet
eating her curds and whey
Three blind mice,

She tells them of kittens,
and mittens, and mice,
Miss Muffet, her tuffet,
and sugar, and spice.

They rap to the rhyme
of "The Cat and the Fiddle."
Poor Rory forgets
all the words in the middle.

"Stretch up high," honks Miss Bingo.

“Now stretch way down low.”

Oh, no! Someone tramples
on Annabelle's toe!

And Annabelle howls,
and Annabelle hops,
and Annabelle sobs,
and storytime stops.

Rory shouts, “Annabelle!
Annabelle! Look!”

And he reads her a rhyme
from the Mother Goose book.
"Hickory-dickory-dickory-dock,
Annabelle Mousey-kin ran up the clock."

He makes Annabelle smile.
He makes Annabelle giggle.

Miss Bingo starts dancing.
"Now everyone wiggle!
Waggle your tails!
Show me your claws!
Flap with your wings!
Clap with your paws
for our storytime hero.
Applause! Applause!"

"Is it time to go home now?"
ask Rufus and Rory.
"No, no," says Miss Bingo.
"It's time for a story."

Mother Goose
Mother Goose

They love it so much
that she reads just one more,

and she blows them a kiss
as they roll out the door.

Now Rory remembers
the cow and the moon,
the little dog laughing,
the dish and the spoon.
And he sings all the words
to his very own tune.

“Toodle-oo, little readers.
Please come again soon.”